THE SURGEON'S SECRETS

A BAD BOY BILLIONAIRE ROMANCE

CELESTE FALL &
MICHELLE LOVE

HOT AND STEAMY ROMANCE

CONTENTS

Blurb   v

1. Samantha   1
2. Damon   6
3. Samantha   14
4. Damon   18
5. Samantha   26
6. Samantha   35
7. Damon   41
8. Samantha   46
9. Samantha   52
10. Samantha   56
11. Damon   61
12. Samantha   64
Sign Up to Receive Free Books   69
Preview of Love Unexpected   71
Chapter One   72
Chapter Two   77
Chapter Three   83

Other Books By This Author   89
Copyright   91

BLURB

Samantha

Dr. Damon Chase just saved my life, going over my doctor's head to perform a life-saving surgery. He's taken me from wondering if I'll die soon to looking forward to my life, and I'm falling for him fast and hard. There are just two problems.

The first one is that the medical ethics board won't look kindly on a senior cardiologist sleeping with any of his patients, let alone a college student just over half his age. The second is that Damon is a man full of secrets. I can sense it. But what can they be? And how can I get him past them, so that I can have him in my arms?

Damon

I'm stuck on a sweet, young thing I saved on the table, even though I know it could get me in a world of trouble. Samantha North. Every time she makes eyes at me, I want to do something about it ...in as many ways and as many positions as she likes.

We're both alone in the world—and I've grown tired of that. I'd consider it more than worth it to risk my professional reputation to have her in my bed and in my life. If that was the only problem, anyway.

But back home in London, I had another life ...a life full of secrets. But abandoning the life of crime that I once led has made me some serious enemies—and that's about to catch up with me. If they find out about Samantha, her life will be in danger. And if that happens, that oath I took to do no harm is going right out the window.

1

SAMANTHA

"Are you sure Dr. Carpenter can't at least take a message?" I plead with the receptionist on the other end of the line. "I know he says that the Verapamil takes some time to take effect, but it's been a week and a half, and I can barely make it to classes."

"I'm sorry," the receptionist says in a bland tone that tells me she couldn't care less. "But his voicemail box is full. He should be back from lunch at 3 PM. If you can catch him before we close, he should be able to advise you."

"So ...when do you close?" I'm trying not to get upset. The pounding in my chest will only get worse if I do.

I try to distract myself by glancing around at the little stand of trees that surrounds me as I sit on a bench at the edge of campus. I started getting dizzy and sick again just walking up a slight incline for a quarter mile, and it scared me.

"We close at 4 PM." She sounds disgusted—whether with me, her boss, or her job, I'm not sure.

"Thank you." I wish that I could reach through the phone and strangle her. Instead, I take a deep, slow breath and struggle to keep my cool as I hang up.

I have to sit there a while as the stress sends a fresh wave of dizziness through me. I'm barely holding back my panic, which I know will only add to the problem. Even then, a few tears roll down my cheeks.

The pills aren't doing anything. I need real help and expertise. Not that cheap doctor who just throws drugs at everything!

The problem started six months ago: bouts of painfully fast and sometimes irregular heartbeats, with dizziness, weakness, and exhaustion. Dr. Campbell keeps trying different pills on me. But even high doses of beta blockers barely put a dent in my symptoms.

My scholarship includes student medical coverage. Unfortunately, it's low-bidder garbage, and Campbell is the only cardiologist in town who takes it. He and his receptionist team have a habit of treating me like dirt when I can least handle it.

Just calm down, Sam. It will get worse if you don't.

This is getting humiliating. In my freshman year I was zipping around campus on my bike like it was nothing. Now and again I would feel a little dizzy, but I was used to that. I've dealt with it my whole life.

Then the attacks started happening. The first time, I was just coming down for breakfast in the dorm cafeteria, ready to face my very last day of finals in my freshman year. I remember walking downstairs to the dorm lobby and stopping short, growing suddenly dizzy as my heart pounded violently.

It's gotten worse since then. Now I shuffle around like an old woman and spend too much of the money I earn at my part-time job on cab fare to get home. I even had to quit my weekly swims.

I can't even soak in the hot tub anymore—and that used to be my number one way to relax. But, now, the hot water will make me even dizzier, as it drives up my already overactive heart rate.

Dr. Campbell claimed recently that I'm not getting better because I'm not taking my meds. I had to get a test to prove to him that my bloodstream is full of the damn drugs; they just aren't doing shit. His response was to try a different set of drugs, which, again, do very little.

I get up and lift my art bag, an old, gray, canvas messenger bag covered in spatters of oil paint, smears of pastel and chalk, and smudges of charcoal. I've had it since I was twelve—one of the few gifts I ever got growing up in the foster system. Right now, it feels like it's filled with bricks.

My final class of the day is at six—a night studio where all I have to do is stand there, paint, and try not to fall over. I don't even have to wrestle any of the big canvases today—it's all five-minute speed sessions on paper. I'll grab a light meal, drink something without any caffeine in it, go up the hill, and throw on my smock.

I'm feeling better after a meal and some fluids. I keep trying the doctor until four, but he makes no effort to return my call. "He has other patients," the receptionist says without apology, while my heart beats so fast and hard it nauseates me.

I wonder if this callous bitch of a receptionist has ever gotten really sick in her life. If things keep getting worse, I'm going to end up in the emergency room again. I already have a huge bill from last month that I can't pay, and the prospect of facing yet another one makes my heart beat even faster.

I agonize over that possibility while I sit on that bench and call Campbell twice more before his office closes. Tears start running down my cheeks after I hang up the second time, and I wipe them away sternly. *Enough of that.*

I didn't get this far by giving up or feeling sorry for myself. I'll find some way to survive this, just like I survived foster care, public school, and getting my ass into college on a full ride. But as I get up and start walking at a painful snail's pace toward the student center, I'm scared to death.

I spend a lot of my time on campus alone. I'm kind of used to it. In school, I was the kid with no parents, who went home to an institutional cot and food that was marginally worse than the stuff in the dorm cafeterias.

Making friends is a new skill for me. Here, at least, classes are so huge that nobody notices that I'm recycling through the same half-dozen outfits every week. But it doesn't make approaching people any easier.

Still, when I get back that evening, completely drained and with paint smudges on my hands, I exchange greetings with a few people on my way up to my dorm room. The guard station and a lot of the dorm doors are decorated for Christmas—mostly cheap, printed, paper decorations, tinsel garlands, and sometimes a string of colored or silver LED lights. The bulletin board on my floor is full of seasonal party announcements.

I try to ignore them and just make it to my door. The sight of them tends to leave me depressed.

I was lucky enough to have been assigned one of the rare single rooms. The room is tiny and plain, but it's the first private room I have ever had in my life, so I refuse to complain.

It's not even eight, and I know that if I sleep now, chances are I'll end up getting up at some weird hour. But I can barely keep my eyes open, so I don't really care. It's bedtime.

I leave my bag and clothes in a pile, pull on a huge, purple t-shirt and shorts, and crawl under the covers, barely remembering to set my phone on the bedside table. If I sleep long enough, the pain in my chest may actually go away for a while.

I wake up hours later to total darkness. I feel like a huge weight has dropped onto my chest. My heart is galloping like I'm running a race, making me dizzy and sick. I gasp and try to sit up, but it hurts too much. *Oh my God, am I dying?*

I flail for my phone and almost knock it off the small table before managing to grab it. Every single heartbeat pounds in my head, my chest burns and aches, and the sides of my neck hurt, like my veins are going to burst.

I manage to dial for help, but everything after that gets vaguer and vaguer. I give my name, location, and information about my heart condition, but it sounds like my voice is coming from far off, as if someone else is in control of it. It feels like I'm drifting further and further from my dorm room, out over a black sea, where the pounding of my heart is all I can hear.

I hang on through sheer force of will as the 911 dispatcher keeps me on the phone and tries to help me stay conscious. The whine of sirens echoes toward me from afar. Then, the darkness closes over my head, and I hear rather than see my phone drop to the floor.

2

———

DAMON

I'm dreaming about the night of the heist again when my phone goes off and drags me straight up from the depths of sleep. One minute I'm jumping into a bank vault while the explosion drops the entire building around me, and the next, my eyes are opening in my posh Chicago penthouse and I'm fine. Except, of course, that my phone woke me up at three in the fucking morning, and who wants to deal with that?

I check the text and immediately sit up. "Shit."

There's a college girl in the ER with some kind of severe heart issue. Her cardiologist isn't returning his calls, and since I'm the cardio man on call tonight, it's time for me to hop to it. I leap out of bed and head for my closet, grumbling curses the whole time, but ready to get my game on.

The *new* game. The one where I'm saving lives instead of chasing cash and trouble back in London. New game—new name, new identity, new life. And I have work to do.

I text the desk nurse back as I take the elevator down from the penthouse. *How are her vitals?*

She gets back to me quickly. *Rapid, irregular heartbeat, with dizziness and pain in her temples, chest, and the sides of her neck.*

She's diagnosed with congenital arrhythmia and tachycardia, the latter presumed to be anxiety-related. She's on a calcium blocker and a sedative.

Arrhythmia? There are many kinds of arrhythmia, and it doesn't bode well that her doctor hasn't put an exact diagnosis on her chart. *What's her electrophysiology study say about it?*

She hasn't had one. Her insurance barely covers the specialist, and her doctor wouldn't do it pro bono. She would have had to pay for it out of pocket.

"Which, of course, she can't fucking do because she's a dirt-poor college student. Fuck," I mumble under my breath. I step out of the elevator into the garage and head for my black Prowler. "I hate for-profit medicine so damned much."

I slide into the driver's seat and text back. *All right. Stop the calcium blockers, keep her calm, and introduce the following into her IV cocktail.* I give a list of three drugs I know they have on hand. *We're going to need to do that study as soon as she is stable enough.*

We'll get it done. ETA?

Ten minutes, barring traffic. Whose name is on the chart as her specialist? I have my suspicions, but I still grit my teeth when she confirms them.

Campbell.

"Fuck." Adrian Campbell is the worst, most negligent cardiologist in Chicago. The two of us are colleagues, but every time I run into him at a conference, I want to punch him in the face.

I've never met a man who mixes arrogance with incompetence as thoroughly as Campbell. He always has at least three malpractice cases pending, and he's killed more patients than he's saved. That girl is as good as dead if she stays in his hands.

Going to have to do something about that, I think to myself.

I put my phone down and strap in, then start the engine and go roaring out into the street. It's chilly out; early December hasn't put snow on the ground yet, but I keep an eye on the road, wary of black ice.

Chicago on the cusp of winter reminds me a bit of London, though the streets tend to be wider and more organized, and the weather's more changeable. Bits of rain spatter my windshield, making tiny, distracting taps against the glass. The streets aren't quite deserted, even at this hour; a few people fight the wind in flapping raincoats as I drive by.

It's Christmas season again, which usually leaves me a bit melancholy. It's not like I can call my family back in London, let alone see them. The colored lights and the wreaths on the lamp-posts are just another reminder that I'm out on my own here in the States.

I speed where I can on the way to the hospital, but keep it sane. I'm not some twenty-something idiot behind the wheel of my first sports car any longer. I just feel a strange urgency with this particular patient, maybe because she's young.

Nineteen-years-old with heart problems. *What a fucking bad hand she has been dealt.* Barely old enough to vote and she's dealing with an issue most folks don't have to face until their sixties or beyond.

I make my way into the staff parking section and ease the Prowler into my space, making sure to lock up before hurrying over to the ER. My foot slips slightly on a patch of ice outside the entrance, and I bite back a curse. I rarely swear on hospital grounds.

"Morning, Dr. Chase. You're in early," Tom, the security guard, greets me.

I give him a distracted nod hello. "Emergency. Some nine-teen-year-old girl's down with a congenital heart problem. Time to pop in and roll up my sleeves."

"Nineteen? Damn. Well, I'm sure you'll be able to help her." He smiles and buzzes me in, and I hurry through.

It's a slow day in the emergency department. The waiting room, with its slowly blinking lights and silver tinsel tree, only has two people, and though every treatment room is full, only one of them has nurses rushing in and out. I feel my heart sink when I see them scurry. *You didn't code while I was on my way, did you, darling?*

"Dr. Chase!" One of the senior nurses, a skinny, bespectacled, older woman named Sarah, bustles toward me with an armful of files. "Thanks for coming so quickly. She's down here."

This is the only place in the world where a guy gets thanked for that. I keep my filthy thoughts to myself as I follow her to the curtained-off room for my first look at Samantha North.

"We've got her stabilized. She's been coming in and out of consciousness. We're prepping for the study now." We go in past the curtain, and I blink down at my new patient.

Shit. The girl's half my age, vulnerable, likely terrified, and very much needs for me to focus on my work right now. But as I walk over to the bed and look down at her, I realize that focusing is going to be a bit difficult.

She's a complete knockout. On the tall side, with milky skin, wavy, red hair, full lips, and a body that looks hot even in a hospital gown. Her breasts are half-uncovered so we can attach the sensors and defibrillate quickly if we must, and I have to tear my eyes away.

For fuck's sake, Damon, get your mind out of her panties and set to work on saving her fucking life! I look over her vitals, then check her chart once Sarah hands it over. "Question. Is her heart rate going back up no matter what drug is being used?"

"Looks like it, yes." She looks over my shoulder at the chart, then turns the page and points to the EKG readouts. "Sedatives helped some and beta blockers helped some. The calcium blockers didn't seem to do anything at all."

"It could be worse than that. Some arrhythmias respond

negatively to calcium blockers. That's why I had you stop them. The study will show us more of what is going on."

I purse my lips and then hand the chart back to Sarah as I go on. "It's possible that she may need laparoscopic surgery before this is over. I'll drive the scope myself. See if they can keep the operating room on standby after they run the study?"

She smiles and nods, seeming relieved. How many times had she tried to call that damned idiot, Campbell, before she gave up and called me? Not too many, I hope.

The poor girl stays unconscious through the entire test; just as well, since it involves threading a scope into her circulatory system. The procedure will only leave her with some soreness and a small entry wound, but the very thought of it gives a lot of patients the shudders. Still, it will save her from open-heart surgery, unless everything in her heart is completely fucked up.

I look over her chart as we wait for the results and am surprised to see an insert from Family Services from only two years ago. Yet another reminder that I shouldn't be staring at her tits, especially openly.

No family. Grew up in foster care. Started off life as Baby Doe after being found in an auto wreck that destroyed her presumed parents, but somehow left her without a bruise.

No record of any distant relatives or foster parents. The facility she was in sent her to the same pediatrician until she aged out of the system, and to my relief, they've sent a copy of her medical records. Dr. Marsh did a much better job in tracking her health issues than the student clinic or, of course, Dr. Campbell.

Reported incidents of light-headedness back through the age of ten. Believed to be anxiety-related, but she has neither a formal anxiety diagnosis nor a diagnosis of PTSD. *And yet doctors keep treating her for anxiety anyway, telling her that what she's been feeling since she was a kid is all in her head.*

If there's one thing I hate more than incompetent doctors, it's prejudiced doctors. The sort who go in assuming they know what's what because their patient is a fat guy, or a smoker, or a young woman. Every body is different, and though certain types tend toward certain conditions, diagnosis and treatment are never one-size-fits-all.

The girl, who's now resting in a nest of wires, sensors, and tubes, her heart still going too damned fast, needs precision as much as she needs empathy. I can offer both, though I can already tell that this one's going to wreck me if she passes. Occupational hazard; I accept it just as I once accepted that I wouldn't live past the age of thirty-five.

Half an hour later, I have my answers. I want to talk to the girl before we actually go in and fix the matter, so she knows what is going on. But I'm determined to do the surgery tonight, before Campbell can make any more of a mess of this.

I have them lower the sedation level so she has a better chance of waking up quickly and then have them watch her until she does.

Not long after, they summon me back to her bedside. I walk in, putting on the best fucking bedside manner I can muster before dawn and my first cup of tea. "Miss North? I'm Dr. Chase, the on-call cardiologist."

Her eyes widen as she takes me in. Even in the midst of her terror, I catch an ember of something I didn't expect in her expression. Time enough to discuss that later, though. "Hi," she manages in a breathless voice.

"Hi there. I'm very sorry about meeting you under these circumstances, but I do have some good news for you, if you feel up to hearing it." I catch myself smiling a bit too much and dial it back, chastising myself.

"Good news is pretty welcome about now. I'm guessing I'm ...out of danger, then?" She forces a tiny, brave smile.

I'm arrested by it briefly, then cough into my fist, trying to cover my lapse. "Yes, well, we performed the test that Campbell neglected to give you, and I can now explain to you what is going on in your heart and how we are going to fix it."

"Oh?" She makes the mistake of trying to sit up and almost immediately stops, wincing in pain at the effort. "Damn."

"Well, we haven't patched you up yet, so don't get too impatient to jump out of bed," I joke with her gently. She offers that brave, charming, little smile again.

"So ...what's wrong with me?" Her voice only shakes a little.

"It's called Wolff-Parkinson-White Syndrome. As you told our nurse that you suspected, it is not treated with calcium channel blockers, such as Verapamil. In fact, they're contraindicated. They can make the situation worse."

She's got one hell of a malpractice suit to bring against that bastard Campbell for his misdiagnosis and mistreatment of a life-threatening disease. I am so sick of his shit that I decide to help her if she'll accept the offer. "We took you off the drugs, and I want you to stop taking them when you get home."

She nods quickly. "Yes, doctor. Should I get rid of them?"

"No. Keep them and decide whether you want to take legal action once you are feeling better. You can use them to support your case, since he put you on something that probably made things worse." I look at her and feel a stab of alarm as her eyes tear up.

"I knew it," she said in a shaky voice. "I knew something was wrong. He and his staff weren't listening."

"I'm afraid that Dr. Campbell is somewhat well known for that. Unfortunately, those on campus health insurance don't exactly have their pick of specialists." She nods, still teary-eyed, and before I can stop myself, I reach out and put a hand on her shoulder.

She stops shaking at once and the waterworks slow. She

looks up at me and smiles sadly. "So what does this syndrome do, and how do we stop it?"

"Well, the short explanation is that the heart has nodes that send electrical impulses through it and tell it when to contract. You happen to have too many of those nodes. They fire at their own rates, and for much of your life, they were likely firing almost in sync with one another. That means they were telling your heart to contract at the same time.

"That means for most of your life, your heart beat like a normal heart. Sometimes the two signals would get out of sync and you would get dizzy, but they likely always went back into sync with one another.

"But, somehow, this year, the two signals went out of sync, and now each one is telling the heart to beat at different times. And your heart is beating extra fast and unevenly to keep up with what the signals tell it to do."

I watch her face as she struggles to digest what—despite my simplifying it as much as possible—was a standard-issue doctorly info-dump. She looks thoughtful, then raises her head to look at me.

"Okay. Thank you for figuring that out for me. Now ...how do we fix it?"

3

SAMANTHA

I'm about to trust my life to the hottest doctor I have ever seen—and I've had my share of medical emergencies. Holy crap, though, this guy ... Looking at him almost takes my mind off the fact that he's going to thread a weird robotic tentacle through my veins.

He's got some kind of British accent—more working-class than Oxford—but despite that, he looks Mediterranean. His wavy hair is almost jet black, and he has it pulled back into a short ponytail at his nape. He has olive skin, liquid brown eyes, and a Roman nose above a wide, well-shaped mouth.

He's tall and broad-shouldered under that white lab coat, and even in my drugged haze, I can't help but notice that he moves like a panther. But most of all, he's got me captivated because he has the answers, because he cares enough to do his job right, and because he's about to fix my problem instead of just throwing pills at it.

The surgical theater is small, and computer screens and equipment dominate one of its walls. I lie on the table while the anesthesiologist prepares my deep sedation. Meanwhile, Dr. Chase is walking me through what's going to happen next.

"Radio frequency ablation is not a long process. We already went in once to run the test, and it will be a simple matter to go in again. I'd estimate half an hour to go in with the laparoscope, and then we'll monitor you until tomorrow."

"That's it? You're telling me that I could be well by tomorrow morning." I can't believe what I'm hearing. No more pills? No more dizzy spells? No more being afraid my damn heart will give out?

"Well, more or less. You'll need to take it easy for about a week after everything you have been through, but normally, this is an outpatient procedure. We'll cause the extra electrical node to stop sending signals using radio waves, and then you're done." He checks my vitals, then makes a few notes. "Right, well, I should go get ready. See you when you wake up!"

The anesthesiologist, a tiny Filipino woman with graying roots, smiles at me and gives Dr. Chase a nod. "All right, sweetie, I'm going to put this in your IV port, and it's going to make you very relaxed. You won't actually remember anything afterward."

"So, like when I got my wisdom teeth out?" I'm nervous, but this is going to happen; it has to happen. And pretty soon I'll be too high to care about what's going on anyway.

"Like twilight sleep, yes." She takes a syringe and slowly empties the milky fluid inside into my IV line. "And here we are. Now, I'd like you to count back from one hundred for me."

"Okay," I say, feeling a different sort of dizziness. A warm rush seems to be riding through my veins. "One hundred ...ninety-nine ...ninety-eight ...ninety-seven ...."

"Uh?" I wake up in a small recovery room, feeling a little bit of pain on the inside of one thigh. I'm sleepy and a little queasy, and the pain is completely gone except for that ache in my upper thigh. I lie there blinking, shocked by the loss of time and memory, even though I was warned.

My heart is beating slowly as the monitor beeps along. It

picks up as I notice it, but not by much. I don't hurt; I take a huge breath and my chest doesn't ache. I have no trouble filling my lungs with air, something I haven't been able to do in a long time.

Intrigued, I press two fingers against my pulse to double check. It feels ...normal. Even. It's not racing at all.

Holy crap. He got it! Dr. Unexpected British Hottie actually fixed me!

All I can do is lie there and stare at the ceiling for a while, grateful tears leaking down the sides of my face. I'm not going to die. *I'm going to be okay.*

And I have Dr. Chase to thank for it.

The door opens, and I look up—expecting a nurse—but it's him, and he's smiling like he's trying not to gloat. "How are you feeling?" he asks, his eyes twinkling.

"Much better," I breathe. "Is that ...is that it?"

"Once you're discharged, I'll want to see you in my office in about a week. I'll make sure you're given an appointment card with directions." He puts his stethoscope in his ears and warms the business end with his hand before laying it above my left breast.

He smiles after a moment. "Deep breaths?" I oblige, and he withdraws, nodding. "Yeah, I'm ninety-eight percent certain that this is sewn up. As is your leg, which may be sore for a few days."

"Thank you, doctor," I say, managing to stop my eyes from leaking again. "I don't know what I would have done ...." I trail off, because I *do* know. I would have died, and it would have been at least partly Campbell's fault.

The thought sobers me a little, but not because it scares me. Now that I can think beyond the possibility of dying, I'm thinking about the possibility of *suing.*

"Don't think of it. You'll be fine now if you look after yourself for a few days." His voice goes from professional to almost tender, distracting me from my growing anger.

I sigh and sit up easily this time. He reaches over and adjusts the backrest for me. The little bit of extra care makes me smile, but it feels unnecessary—I already feel better than I have in months.

"I have to think about it, though," I admit. "Because I'm gonna go sue the crap out of Dr. Campbell once I'm well enough."

He chuckles, and there's a dark gleam in his eyes now, intriguing me. I stare back at him, tilting my head, and he finally says, "You know, I'm absolutely done with that idiot as well. Would you like some help with lawsuit preparations?"

My heart leaps. It has plenty of reasons to leap—he has healed it, he wants to help me even though he doesn't have to, and ...he *is* hot as a Chicago summer. Smiling, I reply, "I'd like that."

4

———

DAMON

I can't wipe the smile off my face by the time I make my way back home. Saving anyone's life is always one for the win column, but Samantha ...well. That girl is special.

TOO DAMN YOUNG FOR ME, but I'm still pretty smitten. I know I'm offering help because a part of me just wants to keep her around for a bit longer. And thanks to pure happenstance, I know that she wants to keep me around as well.

THE FUNNY PART is I know she is quite interested, but I have doubts about taking advantage of that knowledge. I'm not supposed to know she's interested—that information slipped out while she was drugged. She got very ...chatty ...while sedated. Of course, she won't remember it now.

"OH, wow, you're so hot! Are you single? Do you want to go out with me now that I'm not gonna die?"

· · ·

IT WAS ABSOLUTELY ADORABLE. The nurses and my colleague, Dr. Pinoy, all giggled, and I grinned and acted embarrassed and awkward—all the while hoping no one noticed that I was hard as hell. And my expression made my staff giggle more.

BUT I DIDN'T SAY no—only that I would think about it. And I am thinking about it as I drive home ...a lot.

BEING A DOCTOR, I see a lot more of my patients than members of pretty much any other profession. Not just their guts or the insides of their veins, but more skin than most people would prefer—including me, sometimes. And tending to Samantha, I saw quite a bit.

A PERFECT BREAST that I had to ignore, the curve of her inner thigh as I inserted the catheter, and the smooth slope of her belly as the nurses adjusted her draping. Her obvious sex appeal was a distraction, but I fought it off and did the work to save her life, without looking at or touching her inappropriately.

At any other time, the sight of the flawless, silk-skinned globe of her breast would have driven me to at least try flirting with her. There was no ring on her finger. There was no worried boyfriend in the lobby, and she had even asked me out.

ONLY PROBLEM IS, I'm her doctor. I can end up before the medical board on ethics charges if I'm fucking her and treating her at the same time. Even once I'm done treating her—which will be in a week—it could cost me my position. If it gets out, anyway.

I HAVE an excuse to see her, but not an excuse to sleep with her. Just the thought of sleeping with her drives me a bit crazy. Last time I felt this turned on by a woman was years ago, with Molly back in London—in fact, Samantha heats me up even more.

NOT GOING to do a thing about it unless she's vocal about being into it, though. Sometimes what a lady is open to trying when she's drunk on some inebriant is not what she's ready for when she's sober. I may be a rogue and a bastard, but not when it comes to women—or my patients.

THERE'S something bleak about driving back home during the morning commute hours. I've done it many times over the years, usually because I was in on an ER consult or emergency surgery. And before that, there was all the times with my crew back home in London.

I CHECK the clock on the dash: it's 8 AM. "Damn my luck, none of the pubs are open." I hate coming home with my cock hard and my stomach empty.

I COULD HAVE USED a hot meal and a pint or two at Monk's, but I'll have to settle for ordering something up. At least a lot of delivery places in Chicago do morning hours. I am, and have always been, a disaster in the kitchen.

. . .

I GET BACK to the penthouse and start looking up pizza places. Chicago-style pizza is, without doubt, the best in the world. I order a large, all-meat, extra cheese—the sort I'd nag my patients about if it wasn't usually their sedentary lifestyle that was fucking them up anyway. I'll burn off that beast of a pizza in the gym between today and tomorrow, which is about how long it will take me to finish it.

I pour brandy into my tea, throw a dollop of honey into it, and settle into an overstuffed, brown, velvet chair in my living room to await my delivery. I've already told the doorman to receive the pie and how much to tip. I'll save my bottle of IPA to drink with my pizza.

MY SCHEDULE'S off and I could use a nap, but I'm lucky to have nothing else going with work today until this evening. The only possible reason they'll call me in is if they need another emergency heart consult or fix, and that doesn't happen every night. I'm not needed for the average heart attack or gunshot wound.

THE PIZZA PLACE is six blocks off, and they know how much I tip, so I get my pie in well under half an hour. I'm setting it on the table and opening the box lid for that first whiff of scented steam when my phone goes off.

ANNOYED, I scoop it up and see from the screen that it's Dr. Campbell's office. "Oh, hell," I growl, already annoyed with the man, and especially so for his popping up now. Taking a deep breath, I force myself back into my doctor's demeanor and answer the call.

"This is Dr. Chase. May I help you?"

"Dr. Chase." Campbell has one of those dull, nasal, whiny voices that never seem to change pitch much. "I understand that you have taken over the care of one of my patients."

I can tell he's annoyed, even past his bland demeanor. It's all I can do not to grin. *Yeah, I did, and she's going to sue your sad ass, and I'm fucking well going to help her.* "I'm sorry, could you be a bit more specific?"

The truth is—and he damn well knows it—that I am on-call at the ER four nights a week because I spend so much time cleaning up Campbell's messes. His poor suturing, inability to properly direct nurses, and corner-cutting have often left me fighting for the lives of his patients.

I have even lost a few, which I despise him for, because all but one could have been saved if Campbell had done his job.

"Her name is Samantha North. Age nineteen, height five-foot-seven, red hair. You performed an ablation on her this morning at six."

· · ·

FUNNY how the fucker can rattle off details about her with no problem when he's feeling territorial, but he barely did a thing to help her when she needed it. "Oh yeah, the college girl who turned up with Wolff-Parkinson-White."

THERE IS A LONG PAUSE. "I did not make that diagnosis."

"RIGHT, well, that's because there was no electrophysiology study done on her. Otherwise, I'm presuming that you wouldn't have had her on the Verapamil, since it's contraindicated for her condition." I am smiling a hard, predatory smile that makes my cheeks hurt.

FUCKER. You and I both know you're incompetent and don't care to improve. I came up out of the gutters of London a complete miscreant, and I care about your patients more than you do ... all right, especially if they're hot. I'm not anywhere near perfect, and I know it.

HE PAUSES AGAIN. I almost wish I could see his face. Finally, he coughs. "I see. So the ablation was done on an emergency basis?"

"THAT *WAS* what they summoned me to the ER for, yes." It's like he doesn't even realize how much of a fool he is currently making of himself. I wonder in a fit of charity if he's had his coffee yet.

.   .   .

"You realize that you are not in the system for her student insurance, so why did your assistant schedule her for the follow-up consult?"

I wince. I hate how much the damn nurses gossip and how far and fast that gossip spreads. I'm sure it's one of his receptionists funneling the information to him, as no one else can stand him.

"Nora scheduled her because I'm finishing what I started. I'll be taking her on pro bono. You'll no longer have to worry about anything to do with her." My voice is warm, friendly, and reassuring. I don't want him suspecting that I'm going to be helping Samantha bring down a load of karma on him.

"Oh! Well, fine. If you feel like taking one of my charity cases off of my hands, I'm not going to complain."

Charity case? That pisses me off for some reason, and I bite back a response. Forcing myself to calm down, I smile again and keep my tone so sweetly pleasant that he'll miss the bald-faced lie. "Yes, this should be the last you hear about her heart issues, except for a note for your files."

"Thank you for the reassurance," he says obliviously and hangs up.

"That and the fat fucking lawsuit you'll be facing once I help that girl get everything together," I swear as I set my phone back down. *I can't wait to see his face when we nail him on this together.*

I'M good and angry when I go back to my tea, which has cooled too much. I take a few tepid swallows and scowl, thinking hard about what I will need to do to help Samantha build a case. But before I can grab myself some pizza, I catch a glint of light out of the corner of my eye.

MY HEAD SWIVELS on instinct and my eyes fix on the high-rise parking structure across the street. Its top floor is level with my penthouse, giving me an easy, if distant, view of it. There's a man standing at the front edge of the parking structure, up against the railing, facing me.

ALL I CAN TELL about him is that he's big, even taller than me, and dressed in dark colors. I catch that gleam from him again, but before I can go for my telescope or the binoculars hanging over the mantel, he turns and starts walking away. He walks with a slight limp, and I'm left wondering if it was just coincidence or something else.

5

SAMANTHA

I can't get tired of taking my pulse, or walking fast, or taking huge breaths of air. My upper thigh hurts on one side, where the scope went in, but I don't care. I'm recovering fast ...and completely. It's like Dr. Chase flipped a switch inside me.

I'M ALL SMILES. I'm brimming over with joy and vindication. I'm full of defiance as well. *Fuck you, Death. Fuck you, Dr. Campbell. I found the right man for the job, he fixed the problem, and neither one of you is going to see me until I'm damn good and ready —except in court!*

I WANT to dance my way out of the hospital entrance and past the big tree loaded with charity envelopes. I settle for a fast walk, amazed at how my heart doesn't race.

I'M GOING TO LIVE.

It's five in the afternoon and the long twilight of early winter is starting to stretch the shadows out around me. A golden tinge of sunlight shows through the low clouds. The wind bites and I shiver, my delight dampened a little by reality. I have no shoes except for the slipper socks provided by the hospital, no coat, and no money for a cab.

I PAUSE under the overhang and flinch back from a gust of wind. *Oh crap.* The hospital is at least twenty blocks from my dorm, and it's forty-five degrees out.

I MIGHT MAKE IT, but it's going to hurt, and I'm fresh out of the hospital. If only I'd been able to grab my wallet on my way out of the dorm on a stretcher. But I wasn't conscious.

BEFORE I CAN BRACE myself to take my first steps home, I look up —and to my surprise, I see a black Prowler driving toward me. It pulls up at the curb and the window slides down, revealing Dr. Chase leaning toward me from inside.

"BIT COLD FOR STOCKING FEET," he says with a soft smile.

Now the flips taking place in my stomach turn a lot more pleasant. I walk up to the car and can't help but smile back. "Yeah, I, uh ...could use a ride home."

HIS SMILE WIDENS, without looking predatory. "Get in, then."

. . .

THE WAY I grew up has given me a good radar for creeps, and it's not being set off, so I open the door and slip into his passenger seat. It's warm and dry, and the seat I settle my back against radiates heat into my muscles.

"THANKS. That's another one I owe you." I sigh in relief as I buckle up. "I'm in the dorms. I'll direct you."

"ARE you particularly eager to go back there? Though if you wish to rest up alone, I can hardly blame you." He glances at me curiously before pulling away from the curb.

I LIFT AN EYEBROW, wondering about his alternative. "I've been sleeping for hours. I'm just starved." I want to load up on grease and protein right now, even if it isn't the healthiest choice.

"Do you like all-meat pizza?" he asks, and I shoot him a surprised look before nodding. The corners of his eyes crinkle. "Good, because I've one I can pop in the oven if you'd like to come by. I ordered it for myself, but then I got busy with paperwork."

"DON'T TELL me you have details for this malpractice suit already." My eyebrows go up. This guy must *really* dislike Dr. Campbell if he's this dedicated about my lawsuit.

"ACTUALLY, yes. Just some starting stuff but ...he called and made a bit of a nuisance of himself, and after that and what you went through, I was more than a bit motivated." He pulls out of the lot and into traffic. For a moment, his tone turns grave. "You're not the only person he's nearly killed with his negligence."

"So he's the anti-you, then?" Campbell seems to be pompous, aging, incompetent, and lazy. Whereas Dr. Damon Chase is ...amazing.

"Pretty much, yeah." He snorts. "Believe me, even if I didn't like you, I'd still want to see him lose his license to practice. The man's a menace with a scalpel and he's even worse with prescriptions."

"So you do think that I'll have a case?" A mix of anger and hope boils inside of me.

He smirks. "Easily. The man's negligence could have killed you, or, at best, left you with permanent heart damage. He's been sued *sixteen times* for malpractice and settled every time."

"Sixteen times?" I shudder and focus on the hunk next to me to get my mind partway off this horror. *How is he allowed to keep practicing?*

"Yeah, that I know about." He purses his lips. "Look, I'll make you a deal. I'll clear out time a few evenings a week, pick you up, and handle dinner. "We'll get together after your classes and go through everything needed. In return for my help suing that prick, I am going to ask you to put in a complaint with the Medical Board. The more of those he gets against him, the sooner he will lose his medical license, and we'll finally see the last of him."

He winks at me, and I nod back, feeling my determination intensify.

"I don't want him to be able to screw up anyone else's life like this. And I want some of my own back after what he did. This isn't okay." My voice breaks a little.

"No," he replies, jaw set. "It shouldn't be allowed."

We drive. My heart is beating fast—for a reason now—and it doesn't hurt. If anything, this rising excitement makes me feel even more alive than before.

"So how are you doing after resting up? I haven't gotten a chance to look at your discharge file." He deftly maneuvers the powerful car through traffic. *How long did it take him to sort out driving on the other side of the road,* I wonder idly.

I beam. "I feel like I could run a damn marathon. I'm serious."

He looks over at me before heading for the highway on-ramp, his lips quirking. "Well, don't. Or at least wait a week."

· · ·

"I WILL. Don't want to mess up your work. Besides, my thigh feels like I banged it on the corner of a table." I rub it gently through the hospital pants I left in.

"THAT'S COMPLETELY NORMAL. And I hope you're finding it better than open-heart surgery." He winks, and that makes me laugh a little.

"IT'S TRUE. The old way I'd be in recovery for a long time, right?"

"THAT AND, well, it gets a bit gruesome, but you'd need an entire blood transfusion by the time we sewed you up." He merges us onto the highway. I look over and see the gold and pink setting sunlight sparkling across the rippled surface of the lake.

"I'M REALLY glad you have a better way now, then. I just ...look. I owe you a lot—" I start, trying to walk around the issue of how fast I'm becoming infatuated with him. I want to tell him how grateful I am—I've already learned that life is too damned short.

"You owe me nothing," he cuts me off firmly. "Look—is Samantha all right?"

"YEAH," I say after a brief hesitation. "You can call me Samantha." I can feel myself blush shyly at this new familiarity.

"GOOD. Damon's fine here. Look, Samantha, this is my job. Also, I don't feel like this will be over for you until you get some justice. I understand conflict's stressful, but what Campbell put you through was more than just stress." He moves the Prowler into the fast lane and starts whipping along, a hair faster than the cars around him.

IT'S THRILLING to sit in the passenger seat of a car like this and hear the engine revving under me. In a way, my life's in Damon's hands again, and the thought unexpectedly turns me on. I squeeze my knees together, eyes widening as I realize another thing Damon has done for me.

ONE OF THE aspects of my heart problem that I hated the most is that when my chest hurts every time I get excited, it takes all the fun out of sex. I hadn't even had a sex drive to speak of for at least six months. Before that, I was still rebounding from a bottom-of-the-barrel, high school boyfriend who stuck around too long.

THE RIDE FEELS TOO short before Damon pulls us into the underground parking lot of a gorgeous, modern, high-rise apartment building. I stand close to him as we ride up the elevator. He's wearing a little cologne. Something spicy—bay rum, I think.

I STILL DON'T FEEL tired. "It's amazing," I murmur, leaning back against the mirrored wall of the elevator as it rises toward the twenty-fifth floor. "I really think I could stay up for hours longer. I can't remember the last time I felt like this."

. . .

"TECHNICALLY, you won't have. Even if the effects of this anomaly didn't fully manifest until six months ago, it still detracted from your quality of life. But mild discomfort and problems, one can get used to. The level of pain and debility you were experiencing the last couple months, however, couldn't exactly sneak by forever."

SURPRISINGLY, no one else gets in the elevator on the way up, and I hope no one does. I'm happy standing in an intimately small space while alone with him. "No kidding. I was pretty terrified. It felt like I was ...dying."

"WELL ..." He hesitates a moment as the elevator comes to a stop at the top floor. "I didn't want to bring this up until you were fully recovered, but ..."

I STARE AT HIM, my eyes widening slowly. "Then you really did save my life."

"JUST DON'T THINK you owe me anything for it, all right? Saving you was my job. It doesn't imply you have a personal debt to me."

HE KEEPS EMPHASIZING THAT. I wonder why. "Hey, look, I'm just still coming to terms with this. I know it's your job, but that jackass Campbell didn't do his, and it could have killed me."

.　.　.

"I know. It's just that when I'm helping with your heart issue, or any other time I'm wearing my doctor's hat, it's not a favor I'm doing you. This bit with dinner and legal stuff, that's a favor. But not the surgery. You deserved to have someone competent fight for you."

There's something so grim in his expression that I wonder if someone has given him trouble for helping out patients in the past. Or maybe he thinks I'm worried that he will take advantage in some way.

Either way, I'm smart enough to step carefully around the subject if it's a sore point for him. "Sorry, then."

"No, it's all right. I'm happy that things went well and that you're excited about it." His voice goes warm again as we walk off the elevator and into the tiny penthouse lobby, which is decked out with a beautiful skylight ceiling.

I want so much to tell him that I'm getting just as excited about spending time with him as I am about finally being healthy. But when he finally opens the door to his sprawling penthouse, all I can do is stare.

6

SAMANTHA

Polished wood paneling lines the walls, along with an entire wall made from reinforced glass that runs the length of the building on one side. Saddle leather couches in deep brown face an entertainment center that dominates most of a side wall. A balcony enclosed in glass runs all the way around the building, from what I can tell.

"Wow." Other than that, I'm speechless.

His grin is a bit embarrassed. "Yeah, well, I grew up in public housing—council flats, we call them—one of the nastiest areas in all of London. I promised myself I'd get a nice place once I got older." He pauses, then shrugs a bit. "I don't spend much on luxuries outside of the place itself and my car, so I figure I can indulge myself."

"I'm not complaining. This is lovely." Not much in the way of

Christmas decorations, aside from a pine and holly wreath over the entryway that adds a nice odor to the room.

I NOTICE the fancy gas fireplace in one corner and walk to it, extending my fingers to its warmth. There's a single photo on a mantel otherwise dominated by geodes and fossils, and I take a look at it.

IT'S SMALLISH AND OLD, probably thirty years, and creased at the edges behind the glass—as if it was carried in a billfold for a long time. In it, a chubby, gentle-faced woman with curly, russet hair stands in a small, shabby living room with a crucifix on the wall. She wears a cheap, blue, flower-print dress and wraps an arm around two small but already burly boys in ill-fitting, gray school uniforms.

THE BOYS HAVE a similar look to them—one is stockier and thick-featured, with small black eyes and the same mussed, wavy black hair as the other, who has familiar liquid-brown eyes and an easy smile. I look back at Damon as he approaches, smiling at him. "Is this your mom?"

He looks serious suddenly, and my impulse to tease him about having been a really cute kid dies as he stares wistfully past me at the photo. "Yeah, that's my mum and my cousin, Copper, from way back when. They're gone now."

"OH." *Awkward.* "I'm sorry."

.   .   .

"NOT YOUR DOING, sweetheart. I'll pop that pizza in the oven. Like a cup of tea?" He's already headed for the kitchen, which is visible through an archway at the far end of the room.

"YES, THANK YOU." To my surprise, he pulls down a lacquered black tray and a very pretty purple, clay teapot. "That's nice. Chinese?"

"YEAH, Yixing ware. I brew it with black, if that's all right." He starts digging into the cupboard for a tin, glancing back at me.

"THAT'S FINE," I reassure him. I'm not even much of a tea drinker, as I find it bitter and watery compared to a mocha, which is my favorite hot drink. But I don't mind trying his tea if it gives me something to drink with him.

He looks a bit distracted as he puts together the tea service and puts the kettle on. I watch him work—precise as always—his giant hands moving as deftly as a butler's as he slices lemons, pours cream into a tiny pot, and sets a little bottle of brandy on the tray. I've never seen a big, masculine man use sugar tongs before, but he does so without hesitation, sleeves half rolled up.

"HAVE A SEAT ON THE COUCH. I'll be right there," he instructs, pointing me in the right direction. I wander obediently to the gigantic, deeply-padded thing covered in saddle leather.

I SETTLE into it with a sigh, glad for some comfort after dealing with the thin hospital mattress for most of the night. The couch is very comfortable, wide enough to sleep on, and deep enough to sleep two.

OR DO all sorts of things together that I haven't actually ever done, but suddenly want very much to do. With him.

THE DEPTH of my thirst for this man frightens me a little. He saved my life, he's helping me get justice, and he's kind and thoughtful—not to mention dead sexy. He would have made a dead-sexy garbage man, but as it is, the fact that he saves and improves lives for a living makes him even more attractive.

WE KEEP up a steady flow of small talk, getting to know the basics about each other. My work at school. His work at the hospital. Neither of us having family any more—not that I ever had any to begin with.

THE WHOLE TIME my eyes are tracing over his face, his body beneath his black turtleneck and jeans, and those powerful hands that I want to feel on my skin. My eyes keep settling on his lips of their own volition, and I can't help but imagine what they'd feel like on mine. But instead of kissing, we're talking and talking.

HE POURS THE TEA. I drink it with everything, the milk and honey smooth and sweet on my tongue. When the pizza comes out of the oven, dripping with cheese and steaming tomato chunks, it's the best thing I have ever tasted.

. . .

BUT I CAN'T STOP WATCHING him and wondering, *what is it about you?*

We're both on our third slice when his phone goes off. He glances down at it as it lies on the coffee table in front of us and sighs. "Humph, hang on. I keep getting calls from people who aren't on my contact list."

"LOCAL?" I dab at my mouth with a paper napkin.

HE CHECKS ...and then for reasons I don't understand, he goes a little pale. "London." He picks it up. "Hello?"

HE FROWNS and sets it down after a moment. "They disconnected. Odd." But his troubled expression tells me that he finds it a lot more than 'odd.'

I DON'T ASK about it, and after a while we start talking about the lawsuit, which he promises me is about as cut and dried as these things come. "He'll settle for a large sum. It's how he's able to keep the spotlight off of himself—a big, fat check that he tries to use to buy silence. Thing is, he can't make your approaching the board into a condition of the settlement. That's a different matter from the lawsuit altogether." He smiles and pours me another cup of tea. It's actually good, making me wonder what trick he's using to keep it from being so bitter.

. . .

SHAKING thoughts of the tea from my head, I focus on how I have to tell him of my interest—I have to say something or I'll always regret it. But I keep hunting around for the right words and coming up with nothing.

"IS SOMETHING WRONG?" he asks after a while, as if he's sensing my struggle.

"I ...WAS WONDERING SOMETHING," I admit nervously. My fingers twine together between my knees, and I squeeze them hard enough that the knuckles go white. I've never done this before, and it feels like the long, ticking climb to the top of a roller coaster drop.

"YOU CAN'T DATE your patients, can you?" I don't know how I get the question out. I blush at once, embarrassed at myself and worried that I'm about to be shown the door.

7

DAMON

I can't help but grin at her shy, little question, and that only makes her blush more and cut her eyes away, squeezing her hands between her knees again. God, she's so cute. "Well ...I've got good news and bad news on that score, sweetheart, though I admit you may not think as well of me once I tell you."

"You're married?" she asks worriedly at once. I laugh and shake my head.

"No, nothing like that, I promise. The medical ethics board has a problem with doctors dating past patients and a real problem with doctors dating current patients." I hesitate suddenly. There's another reason she might not want to get close to me.

I've done my best to cut ties and leave my past in London in the past—where it belongs. But I absolutely hate lying to women. It always ends badly, but in this situation, I don't even know where to begin telling the truth or how much is safe to tell.

Well, sweetheart, my mum isn't dead and neither is Copper. The first one, I will never stop feeling horrible about, and the second is so he doesn't find me and fucking kill me. We were both raised up in the family business, you see, and the family business is larceny.

You don't abandon the family no matter what happens, even if staying in the business is killing you. But I had to go, and thanks to a total accident, I got the chance to make away clean with a small fortune. *And if I tell you about how I hurt my mum and Molly by faking my death, well ...if the fact that I'm a thief and a killer doesn't drive you away, that probably will.*

I don't bring it up yet. I don't want to end up pushing too much upsetting stuff on her all at once. Instead, I let the medical board matter sink in and watch as she frowns slightly.

"So you could be fired." She sounds worried.

"Censured, certainly—fired, possibly. With men like Campbell around fucking things up, I imagine they'll give me leeway just for cleaning up his messes. But ..." I lean back in my seat next to her. I have barely touched her yet, but now that she's brought this up, it's a real trial to keep my hands to myself.

"But what? I mean, I don't ...I don't want to get you in trouble." Her pale-gray eyes stare into my dark ones, and I smile and reach out, touching the back of her hand gently.

"You're not getting me in trouble. If I don't handle this properly, *I* could get me in trouble." I want to caress her right now. I want to spend the night exploring each other until we're exhausted. But just looking at her, still half-dressed in her hospital clothes, I know I can't.

"Just believe me, I'd be proposing we do something about this right now if it wasn't for the rules." I glance down at her leg. "And the fact that, young lady, you still have a good deal of healing to do." I give her a wink and a smile, trying to reassure her, but she's blushing again and looking down at her hands suddenly.

Her shyness makes her even more adorable. She's beautiful

and doesn't seem to know it, and her modest, unassuming manner is refreshing.

"You're right," she says with a tiny smile. "I ...know I'm going to see you again since we're going to be kicking Campbell's ass in court. But I ...well, I'd date you even if we had to keep it a secret for a while."

I feel that tentative warmth again. I know I'm not much of a romantic, especially after all the darkness and blood I had to wade through back in London. But I'd love to try it with her anyway.

Maybe. If things go well ...

My cock throbs impatiently inside my jeans, as now I have to fight both desire and affection. Finally, unable to stand it anymore, I lean over and kiss her very lightly.

Her full, sweet lips feel silky against mine, and a touch cooler. I hear her draw a trembling breath, and her fingertips skate down over my shoulder. Then, very reluctantly, I let her go.

"I'll keep that in mind," I tell her, staring into her eyes. "But right now, you need to go back and get some rest."

Driving her back to the dorms and dropping her off a block away is more difficult than I thought it would be. I'm actually getting an ache in my balls from the many times that I've gotten turned on today without release. I think briefly about calling on one of the friends-with-benefits I keep on my roster, but ...I know sex with them won't satisfy me.

I want Samantha. I want to spend time with her. I want to kiss her and hold her in my arms, and when the time comes, I want to spend a whole night satisfying us both. It's such a powerful feeling that it unnerves me a bit. But I can't deny it.

Instead, I make sure she's all right to walk the short distance in her borrowed Wellies. I watch her make the walk, and I watch her swipe her card and go inside the building. And, then, I force myself to go home, knowing that I'm going to need a very stiff drink.

Weeks pass and winter really starts to set in. I start to think about inviting Samantha for Christmas. Neither one of us has a family anymore—herself by accident and myself by necessity.

Samantha and I plot against Dr. Campbell. We work as a team, putting together a timeline of events and collecting paperwork, including her pre-hospitalization medical record, which shows the lack of thorough testing. We get a copy of the prescription for the calcium channel blocker that Campbell had given her, which likely worsened her condition, and we put a plastic bag with the bottle in it in our growing evidence folder.

We have dinner together. I try to impress her at first, but we both turn out to be steak, pizza, and Chinese takeaway people, so I lay the wines and foie gras aside (always hated them both anyway) and we focus instead on enjoying our time together.

We always kiss goodnight, and I always have to fight to keep it from going further. She's healing first, and then, after that, she's scrambling to catch up with classes. I try not to distract her and bury myself in my work a bit to keep from being distracted myself.

I find myself looking for Christmas gifts for her in jewelry catalogs online. I find something perfect and receive the wrapped box in the mail and hide it away in the top of my closet. Then I add a few things—Wellies in her actual size and a good winter coat—and stash their wrapped boxes in the same place.

Finally, on the afternoon of December fifteenth, we go to see a lawyer I hunted down who has won five cases against Campbell by himself. His name is Michael Chang, and he agrees right away to see what we have.

He turns out to be a tallish, lean man with tan, wispy hair that is thinning on top and small, black eyes that remind me of Copper's. The resemblance distracts me, and I avoid looking at his eyes unless he is talking directly to me. Instead, I focus on his little, silver holly-sprig tie tack.

Samantha sits next to me in a plain, navy blue dress that is apparently her best, hiding a fraying section of the sleeve cuff under her wrist. She looks very nervous, and I reach for her hand and hold it as the lawyer looks over our folder.

"This detrimental prescription, the lack of any response to an emergent situation involving chest pains, and the lack of essential testing all point toward an extremely dangerous level of negligence." He turns the last page and sets the folder aside with a small smile. "It's entirely consistent with the other cases I have taken against Dr. Campbell."

"So you'll take the case?" Samantha sounds both worried and eager.

"Oh, absolutely. If I were you, I would high-ball your suit, say to the tune of one million dollars. Chances are that he will offer half that as a settlement."

Samantha goes pale and her eyes bulge. I chuckle and hug her gently. "Don't sell yourself short, dear," I purr in her ear. "He did greatly endanger you and extend your suffering."

She nods and sets her jaw, looking up at the lawyer. "I'm going with your advice on this one."

He sits back with a smile and looks between us. "Good, good. I'll file the paperwork, and we'll see what his lawyer's response is."

I give her hand another squeeze behind the desk, and she shoots me that small, brave smile. I squash another surge of desire. "All right, then. Let's go home and celebrate."

8

SAMANTHA

My stomach flutters as I sit next to Damon in his fancy, black car again. We're driving from my dorm to the highway, cruising under temporary archways of fake greenery and real icicles. Christmas lights and displays shine from every window and lamp post, and the sidewalks are full of bustling shoppers.

Normally, the Christmas season gets me depressed, because I've never had anyone to spend it with. Before meeting Damon, I'd planned to spend my holiday as one of the few people stuck in the dorms for the season. But, instead, I'll be spending it with him.

The last two weeks have been a tremendous thrill. Not only am I feeling better than I have in years, not only are we finally filing the lawsuit after a ton of work, but Damon and I are being romantic as hell, holding hands and stealing kisses. It's all new to me; I've never been touched by a man before, and though we're not doing much yet, it's still amazing.

Every time he kisses me—even the slightest touch of his lips—it both thrills and frustrates me. Under awnings as we escape the rain, under sprigs of mistletoe that seem to have sprouted in every shop doorway, and almost every time we touch, our lips find each other. His mouth is always warm and sure against mine, and when he cradles me against his broad chest, it makes me feel safer than I've ever felt before.

BUT HE DOESN'T GO beyond that. I know that he wants to. Each time, I feel him struggling to control himself.

I WISH that he wouldn't. But with the lawsuit and Board complaint likely to shine a spotlight on the pair of us, the best I can expect until we win are some longing looks and a little tenderness. And none of that in public.

IT STILL MAKES me sad and frustrated. My feelings aren't rational, but it's sometimes like I'm a shameful secret he is keeping. I also feel sometimes that he isn't telling me the whole truth about himself—he's just too good to be true. The random calls from nowhere that he won't answer around me and how tense he gets after them really make me wonder. And, sometimes, he will start telling me a story about his life and then suddenly leave off, as if the story is wandering into parts of his life that he doesn't want to reveal to me. I start to suspect that he does have a wife or a steady girlfriend stashed somewhere.

. . .

IF THAT IS THE CASE, at least he has some ethics to him in not sleeping with me—even if he is still flirting with me and kissing me. Each time he kisses me, my whole body aches with the hunger for more. But, like him, I end up conflicted—mostly because he is, and I don't know why, but my emotions seem to take a cue from him.

I SUSPECT that I am being paranoid about things. He told me his reason for not getting serious with me yet. And still ...I can sense that there's something he isn't telling me—something that might be even more important.

"SO I'M THINKING I'll try some of that sorbet stuff while we're in the hot tub, if you're into it." He has a gleam in his eye and a little curl to his lips.

IMMEDIATELY I FEEL my sex tighten as my nerves come alive from my neck to my knees. Is tonight the night? Is he finally getting so thirsty for me that it's making him reckless? In spite of the risks, I hope so.

"I DON'T HAVE A BATHING SUIT," I point out, and his lopsided smile widens as he takes the on-ramp onto the highway. We both go quiet as he merges with traffic and then starts moving left toward the fast lane.

HE'S SETTLED into the drive and is starting to answer when a white van roars up beside us and starts edging aggressively into our lane. Damon curses and pumps the brakes, letting the van in front of him before it can knock us into the guardrail. It ends up scraping along against the furrowed metal itself, striking sparks along one side.

"OH MY GOD!" I gasp and turn to look at Damon. That didn't look like an accident. He scowls and grips the wheel, his whole expression and demeanor changing in an instant.

I STARE at him in horror as the pleasant, friendly, foul-mouthed, and flirty doctor I know disappears in an instant beneath a cold, hard glare. Even when he speaks, his accent has thickened. "Hold on."

HE TAKES advantage of an opening and swerves to the side, neatly maneuvering the car around the van and getting in front of it. The van speeds up, trying to attack again, but Damon floors it—and the Prowler leaps to life.

THE ROAR of the engine sends my heart racing in a way I have never associated with pleasure before, as an enormous thrill runs through my whole body. We leave the van behind within seconds, as the bulky, weaker-engined vehicle reaches its limit. My terror dissolves in the thrill of escaping.

HE DOESN'T SLOW down or say anything at all until he's left the van far enough behind that we can no longer see it. "That was not some random drunk," Damon finally growls, sounding furious about it. "That was a targeted attack."

"I DON'T UNDERSTAND," I mumble, shivering in fear. "Why would anyone be after me?"

"THEY'RE NOT AFTER YOU, sweetheart, except by association." He sounds resigned, his rough manner and accent only gentling now that he's speaking to me. "They're after me."

IT'S a tense drive back to his penthouse, and I'm too dizzy, baffled, and scared to ask too many questions until we're safely indoors. On the way up the elevator, he looks at me and a touch of the old tenderness returns to his eyes. "You all right?"

"I GUESS I would be a lot worse if you weren't such a good driver," I breathe, not sure what else to say. "But you owe me one hell of an explanation."

HE NODS, his jaw working as he leans his head back against the wall of the elevator. "Yeah. Suppose I've put this off for too long."

WE PICK the chairs closest to the fireplace, and I stretch my hands toward it, feeling the chill and the shivers of fear fading at once.

He brings us both tea with lemon, honey, and brandy and waits until I've swallowed down my first cupful before he goes into his story. The whole time, it's like he's become some gentler version of Mr. Hyde—rough, working-class, hard-eyed—but only when he isn't looking at me.

WHEN HE DOES LOOK at me, his brown eyes go soft again and their gaze fills me with warmth. And that's the only thing keeping me going as I struggle to listen to his story.

9

SAMANTHA

"I told you the truth about being born to a nasty public-housing apartment. And all the rest of it, I gave you a patchwork of truth—with a lot of holes, I admit it—but there wasn't a lie among them." Damon sounds a little guilty, like he's almost desperate to reassure me.

"But what I left out is ...I didn't start out some fancy, white-hat doctor who goes around saving lives. That's my penance for what I did before. It's how I can live with myself now."

He takes a long swallow of his drink and then refreshes it with straight brandy before setting the mug down. "My dad's been doing a stint in Wandsworth—prison—for as long as I've been alive. I've never even met him. But he was still the head of the family business, because without his name I would never have had any dealings with that world."

"What's the family business?" I can guess, but I want to hear it from him.

"Well, my dad managed to get himself forty years for a diamond heist. His younger brother, my uncle, was still knocking over banks and high-end shops, which meant he was in and out of jail as well. The difference was, he had a better lawyer and was usually out within a few months each time.

"So my mum and my aunt moved in together, and that made it me and my aunt's son, Copper, growing up like brothers. My uncle would come by for a few months, dig up cash for us from God knows where, and then get picked up for something and have another round behind bars.

"In between, he started teaching Copper and me things. How to lift a wallet, how to copy a key, how to crack a safe, and how to control a room during a robbery." Damon sits back and swallows down the contents of his mug, then lays it aside with a sigh.

"There were no jobs for young lads when I started out and no money for college. When Copper came to me and said he had a driving job for me, I didn't know I would be driving a getaway car for him and his lads. But, then, there I was, right in the midst of it." He speaks frankly, making no apologies and no excuses.

"I got in too deep before I even realized just how badly off we all were. They were knocking over shops during football riots and breaking into cars during the holidays. I drove them and got them away, and got a cut of the money for it. Copper kept telling me we were like Robin Hood, except this time, the poor we were giving to was us."

I watch his face. The hard expression has gone bleak, replaced by a tortured look filled with regret. Some of the fear trickles out of my heart, but burning curiosity and a little wariness replace it.

"My mother hated it. She cried about it and begged me to stop. And I kept trying. Copper would beat my ass for making him look bad to the others, and I learned to fight properly, so he'd have a harder time doing it."

He eyes the brandy bottle, then shrugs and takes a long pull from it, not giving a damn any more. I'm still on painkillers or I would reach for it myself. As it is, I'm nursing the rest of my mug.

"Then Copper gets mixed up with these guys my uncle's been doing jobs with and not a single one of them is any good. In fact, every last one is rotten. I beg him to leave with me—to just go—but he's in too deep."

He licks his lips and turns toward the window wall, that sad, empty look on his face making my heart ache. "So they decide to graduate to bank jobs. And my uncle decides that this time, I'm going in. They need someone smart and steady-handed to crack the safe.

"I end up in even deeper. Somewhere around my third year of that, we're hitting a bank in Leeds. We end up faced with a safety door that slams down in front of the vault while I'm inside it gathering things up. And the idiot entry man Copper picked up on short notice sets the charges off too close to a gas pipe."

I sit back, astonished, as he winces and nods. "Wow. Did the whole building go up?"

"Yeah, and then it went down. I rode out the explosion and collapse in the vault, grabbed the two million in diamonds we had come for, and disappeared. I hated doing it, but I knew I'd be presumed dead, and that was my only chance to escape."

I just stare at him, my mouth open in astonishment as I process this latest bit of information. "You ...you fled to America then? Got a new identity?"

"Yeah. I did. I left everyone behind. Copper, my mum, my girl —let them all think I'd died. I came here, bought myself a new life, and laid down capital for this building, which paid for itself while I put myself through medical school."

He spreads his hands, sighing. "I've kept my hands off of you because you're a sweet girl, really lovely, and you've had enough people messing up your life. I'm a miscreant, damn it. I've got phone calls from unknown London cell phones and I've got unmarked vans trying to run me off the road. Someone's found me." He reaches out and cups the side of my face in his big hand so tenderly that it brings tears to my eyes.

"I don't deserve you, and sticking around is going to put you in danger. It's not that I don't care for you, Samantha. It's that I do, and I'm poison for you. Especially right now."

It hurts. A shudder goes through me, almost a convulsion, while a stabbing pain runs through my chest. A sob escapes me, and the pain that flashes across his face at the sight of it only makes it worse.

He saved my life twice. He's the only person I have ever had who has really given a damn about me, and I can't lose him— even if staying with him puts me in danger. I can't.

"Shit." He gathers me against his chest, his body tense and his heart beating fast. "I'm sorry. I didn't mean to upset you. I know you've been through a lot, even without me."

"Without you, I'd be dead." My voice comes out surprisingly calm, and he freezes, then slowly looks down to meet my gaze. "Twice," I remind him, before looking away shyly. "Anyway, it's too late. Whoever tailed us onto the highway to attack us already knows I'm mixed up with you."

He sighs and swallows, blinking rapidly. "Damn." After a long, thoughtful silence, he mutters, "I can try and keep you safe. But I don't know how I'm going to make up for dragging you into my problems."

I take a deep breath, steadying myself against him, and then slide my hands up his chest as he looks into my eyes. "You can start by making love to me."

10

SAMANTHA

My heart beats fast and hard and without any pain at all as Damon pushes me firmly against his bedroom wall and buries his face in my neck. His nimble fingers are busy with the row of buttons running down the front of my dress, pushing the fabric down off my shoulders as he goes. My head lolls back against the wall and I whimper as sensations I've never experienced before start rushing through me.

His mouth starts traveling into my cleavage as he frees me from the dress one arm at a time, then pushes the navy-blue fabric down to my waist. He lifts me effortlessly, nibbling at my exposed chest before reaching back one-handed to unfasten the catch of my bra. He's gentle, but fast, leaving me once again with that wild thrill of feeling like I've been pushed past my own control.

I want him to do this, but I don't have the words for it. I don't even know why I want it so badly until his agile tongue darts under the edge of my loosened bra cup and grazes my nipple. I gasp, my eyes gone enormous, and suddenly I'm eagerly pulling off my bra the rest of the way myself.

He runs his knee up between my thighs to support me as he takes my nipple roughly in his mouth. His first long pull makes me whimper loudly and stretch against the wall, my nails clawing his shoulders through his shirt. His grip tightens and he starts sucking again, long, rough pulls that mix pain and pleasure in just the right way.

I try to muffle my cries at first, but after a while, I just can't. He moves from breast to breast, holding me firmly while I arch back against the hard wood, squirm, and clench my legs around his knee. My hips are rolling unconsciously, grinding my pussy against the muscle of his thigh, and finally I get too turned on to care how much noise I make.

My cries rise slowly, long moans growing sharper and louder as he intensifies what he's doing to me. His free hand wanders down to unfasten more buttons, unwrapping me like a present. Under my dress, I'm in a matching set of thigh-high stockings and panties.

He leaves the stockings on. As for the panties, he grips my whole pussy through them and starts kneading me in time to the movements of his mouth. Powerful jolts of pleasure start running up from my groin to mix with the ones his mouth teases from me, and I feel one of my shoes drop to the floor as I lift my feet from the ground.

The other drops as I wrap my legs around his hips, shimmying reflexively as his hand moves between us. I can't seem to keep my breath in my lungs any more. My throat burns, my lungs strain, and yet everything I do and feel is edged with pleasure so intense that it almost scares me.

He groans harshly and grips the panties—then tears the little triangle of damp cloth off me entirely to get it out of his way. I feel his fingers stroking and exploring me, and then his head lifts slowly from my breast as he raises his eyes to mine. He lets out a shuddering breath, then shifts his grip on me and carries me toward the bed.

I sob in frustration as he stops pleasuring me, my body on fire with the need for him to go on. Instead, he throws me onto the bed and leaves me to writhe as he tears off his own clothes. I see a few buttons pop off his dress shirt. When he shoves his pants and boxers down, he gasps with relief.

I see the tool he'll soon be using on me and almost—almost—freeze up. It's big enough that a guy of his strength could tear me up easily. Smooth, sleek, a little curved ...I crave it and feel pretty damn intimidated at the same time.

He grabs me by the hips and drags me toward the edge of the bed, crouching there, and starts stroking my cunt again while he positions himself with his other hand. I close my eyes, forcing myself to focus on the two fingers stroking me just above where he's slowly starting to push inside.

The pressure intensifies the mounting pleasure inside of me instead of drawing away from it, and I gasp in amazement and squirm as he slides deeper and deeper into me. I hear him groan, then feel the muscles in his belly working against me as he sinks in deeper. I look up and see him propped over me on one hand, his eyes closed and his lips parted in bliss.

He leans down over me, covering my body completely, and I grab hold of him with arms and legs and hang on for dear life as his hips thrust deep and push me into the mattress. The bed bounces under me as he drives himself into me again and again; his fingers caress me in time to his thrusts until I'm lifting my hips to meet him. In seconds we've found a rhythm and I find myself riding toward a peak I've never known.

His breath growls harshly in my ear as our bellies slap together. His hand between us trembles but he keeps stroking me. Inside me I feel a fuse being lit—my back arches slowly upward, whole body taut as he pounds into me, and time suddenly slows.

A wave of sensation expands outward from my pussy, so intense that I thrash and wail like he's stabbing me, but I'm crying for more. Torrents of pleasure roar through me over and over, leaving me crying and clawing at his back as he moves almost violently against me.

I croon, shiver, and shimmy against him, rolling my hips to feel him inside me better while he grits his teeth and starts to shout between gasps for air. He speeds up his thrusts, the shouts growing louder and hoarser as I feel the tremble starting in his hips. His hoarse cries and tremors excite me. I feel his surging cock set off aftershocks inside of me that make me whimper again.

He suddenly arches his back hard, pushing me so deeply into the mattress that the bedsprings creak hard. A long, almost agonized groan echoes off the walls as his cock twitches and jerks inside of me. He grinds his hips slowly, his gasping dying down, and then settles over me with a sigh.

We drowse together and make love again as soon as we have the strength—gently this time, slow, and curled on our sides. This time, when I climax, I almost weep with the tenderness of it and realize how much I'm looking forward to more nights like this. We sleep a while, and then I wake up and realize I'm sticky, sore, and desperately want some of our leftover pizza.

When I come out of the shower, I'm reluctant to dress, but without anything else to wear unless I raid his closet, I shove myself back into my bra and dress and step into my shoes. Letting out a sigh, I look down at Damon sleeping quietly ...and then move past him toward the living room and the kitchen beyond.

It's just barely before dawn and I'm still almost too sleepy to walk properly, let alone think. I notice a washing rig on the other side of the window, with a big man in a jumpsuit and hard hat standing on it, doing something to the glass. Whatever it is makes a little screeching sound as he finishes up. Then I hear a sharp snap.

I don't realize that he's using a glass cutter until a big circle of glass falls into the room and shatters, letting in a blast of freezing wind. I let out a scream of shock and horror—and then the big man bulls through the gap and grabs me, clapping one giant, gloved mitt over my mouth.

11

DAMON

Samantha's cut-off cry of panic and horror sends me shooting up from a sound sleep and adrenaline burns through my veins like cold acid. I leap up and run naked into the living room—just in time to see the huge hole in my window and the window-washing rig dropping out of sight. The last thing I see is a huge figure wrapping her in his gigantic coat as she struggles in his grip.

Wrapping her in his coat?

Panic and confusion warring in me, I barely notice the cold biting at my naked skin. I yank on my clothes, throw on my shoulder holster with my .357 in it, and yank my leather jacket on over that. I grab my keys and am stuffing my phone in my pocket when it rings suddenly.

It's a London phone number.

I pick it up at once, and I know who it's going to be. "Copper, you fuck! What the hell are you up to? If you hurt that girl—"

"Nobody's getting fucking hurt," comes the rumble, with an even deeper and thicker accent than I remember. "That's why I'm handling it and not Dad's fucking goons." He suddenly loses a lot of his bravado. "She's fine, Denny. I just can't guarantee she'll stay that way long."

There's a thread of tension in his voice that I notice even through my rage. "You've got one fucking chance to explain yourself, Copper." I grab my rappelling gear from my gym, run out to the stairway, and clip my harness around my hips and thighs. The end of the rope clips to the heavy pipework safety rail.

In the background, I can hear Samantha's muffled cries as she tries to reason with her giant of a kidnapper. The engine for the cleaning rig putters in the background, and I can hear the ropes creak as it lowers. It has to go slowly in this wind. "Copper, I'm warning you. I'll put a bullet in you to get her back."

"What, me? Fuck, Denny, I thought you were some fancy, life-saving doctor now." But his mockery comes out in a weak tone.

"I am. Which should tell you how much she means to me. Don't fucking think I'd feel good about it, but you're not giving me a choice." I test my lines and the harness fastenings and make sure to strap in my pistol securely.

I hook one leg over the railing. "Copper, this isn't like you. You've never dragged innocent people in like this, and don't tell me you've changed that much. So what the fuck is going on? Final chance."

He takes a deep breath and lets it out at once. "Dad sent us round to chase up a rumor that you'd been seen in Chicago. It's me and Ben. When he found out you're alive, Dad lost his shit. He's got my family, Denny. Either I pull that two million out of your hide or he'll kill his own granddaughter. She's fucking two, Denny!"

"Fuck." Suddenly everything in my world makes sense again. "It's just you and Ben?" Ben may have to die. Otherwise, he'll be sticking around making a nuisance of himself, reporting back to Copper's dad if anything happens.

I can't believe that everything shifted so fast on me. I should have seen the signs. That man on the rooftop almost two weeks ago—Copper, with a pair of fucking binoculars, looking in on me. Making sure it *was* me.

"Yeah. But if you fuck this up—" the pressure in his voice speaks volumes.

I scoff. "I could pull two million out of my fucking vault right now. Your dad's an idiot. You could have gotten four million out of me with a polite phone call. I know I caused trouble running off. I just had to get out of the fucking life."

I look down the shaft of the stairwell. "Don't hang up." I stuff the phone in the zipper pocket on the front of my jacket, grab the line, and step out into space. Rappelling in dress shoes is a bit of a trick, but I didn't have time to grab my climbing shoes.

I make a fast descent, bounding from railing to railing while the line pays out, pausing to retrieve and re-clip it twice. In under a minute, I'm on the ground floor. I run out, leaving the harness behind and pulling out my phone.

"You there?" I growl as I race out through the lobby and around toward the side of the building that he's descending. "Where the fuck is Ben?"

"White van—" is all I hear before I see the slightly battered van that had attacked us on the highway go roaring past down the side alley. I run after it, pulling my pistol.

"If you let him hurt her, I'll fucking shoot you both," I snap and hang up. Negotiations are over. Now I have to make sure crazy, trigger-happy Ben doesn't decide to put a bullet in my girl before Copper and I can get him under control.

I see them up ahead—the van is parked under the window-washing rig, which is slowly descending. Praying that I'll make it in time, I run toward them faster than I ever have in my life.

12

SAMANTHA

I'm screaming and fighting with all my strength when the enormous man on the descending scaffold suddenly grumbles something about how I'll freeze to death out here. Before I know what's happening, he's wrapping me in his coat, shocking me into stillness. It's then that I get my first look at him.

"COPPER? Are you Damon's cousin, Copper?" My head spins. Damon talked about this man being torn between his father's crime legacy and their own desire for something better. But I never expected to be face to face with him.

"THAT'S ME," the giant grumbles. "Sorry about that. If it's any comfort, this isn't anything personal at all."

"YOU JUST YANKED me out of a penthouse window and are kidnapping me by transporting me down the side of a high-rise.

How am I not supposed to take it personally?" I look around, terrified to be trapped on this windy, fragile thing.

HE SNORTS and holds me by the scruff, the heavy coat trapping me as much as warming me. I see him put a cellphone to his ear. "Yeah. I've got her. I'll send the ultimatum once I'm far enough down the building that he can't shoot me."

HE LISTENS and his face twists into a scowl. "Yeah, well, you tell my father that if he lays a finger on either of them, I'll kill him myself. Hate this whole fucking business."

SOME MORE LISTENING, and then he hangs up the phone and calls Damon. I try to call out to my lover, but immediately get a huge hand clapped over my mouth again.

BUT LISTENING to the conversation relaxes me slightly. Damon seems to be getting through to this guy—who isn't even acting of his own will. When he hangs up, he removes the hand from my mouth, but looks at me forbiddingly. "No more screaming. Fucking Ben has a hair-trigger."

"Look," I say hastily. "I get that you're being pushed into this, but you should really rethink your approach. Damon owns this fucking building. If you want two million, he could probably just put it together for you."

"YEAH, and were it up to me I'd say yes in a trice. But my dad wants Denny to suffer. Now, if you're careful and do as I say, it shouldn't be a problem." He looks down and scowls as a van roars around the corner and drives up to stop underneath us. "There he is now."

"I SEE HIM." My heart sinks. *The last thing I need is to be stuffed in a van and driven away before Damon can even get down ...stairs ....?*

THE FIRST THING that pops into my head when Damon races around the corner with his cellphone in one hand and his gun in the other is *how the hell did he get down faster than we did?*

A MAN OPENS the van's sunroof. He's redheaded, stocky, and scarred across his cheeks, and has a pistol in his hand as well. "Hurry up you fucking tit. We have to get out of here before someone notices us!"

Then he sees where Copper and I are looking as we descend, and he curses in such a thick Irish accent I can't catch what he's saying. And then, in a moment I'll never forget for the rest of my life—however long that may be—he turns and fires on Damon. With reflexes faster than I've ever seen, Damon ducks behind a dumpster and shoots back. The man grabs his arm, gasping ...but just switches his gun to the other hand.

"YOU FUCKING CALLED him and warned him, you bastard!" the redhead yells up at us—and then he's pointing that huge pistol up at the two of us. "I'll kill you and the girl both!"

"DON'T DO IT, BEN!" Copper booms and shoves me behind him.

I stare at his back ...and down at Damon. In that moment, I truly understand how he and Damon could have been raised as brothers.

THREE GUNS GO OFF AS one, and the giant in front of me grunts in pain and doubles over. I grab him and haul him back with all my strength before he can fall off the scaffold. Once I have him safe and am putting pressure on his chest wound, I look down and see that, though Copper missed, Damon's bullet found its mark. I glance at the red-haired corpse and then go back to tending to my reluctant kidnapper.

"COPPER!" Damon yells, having seen the big man take the bullet for me while he killed the shooter. "You still with us?"

"FUCK," Copper gasped. "Yeah, but don't know how long I'm for it. Think the fucker hit me in the heart."

"YOU COULDN'T TALK if he'd hit you in the heart." Damon climbs up to us. "I've called for an ambulance. Let me do the talking once they get here."

"WELL, IT FUCKING HURTS LIKE IT." The big man's scared. Can't blame him—I was on brink too, recently. Even though he dragged me out of a window in the middle of the night, I grab his hand so he'll have someone's to hold.

· · ·

"Well, you're in luck, because I happen to specialize in fixing hearts." Damon takes off his jacket so we can wrap Copper in his own coat. We hear the wail of the ambulance siren—Damon's credentials get fast results.

"Yeah, he's not kidding. He just fixed mine a few weeks ago." I smile down at the bruiser, whose eyes twinkle weakly.

"Really? Well ...that's really something ...." he mumbles. As he starts passing out, he says to Damon, "Denny ...if I don't make it ...fucking call your mother. It's Christmas."

"I will," Damon promises, slipping an arm around me as we wait for the ambulance crew.

SIGN UP TO RECEIVE FREE BOOKS

Sign Up to Receive Free E-Books and Audiobook Codes.

Would you like to read **The Unexpected Nanny, Dirty Little Virgin** and **other romance books** for **free?**

You can sign up to receive these free e-books and audiobooks by typing this link into your browser:

https://www.steamyromance.info/free-books-and-audiobooks-hot-and-steamy/

Or this one:

https://www.steamyromance.info/the-unexpected-nanny-free/

PREVIEW OF LOVE UNEXPECTED

A Fake Relationship Romance

By Eliza Duke

Synopsis

Nakita had no idea what she was getting into, when she accepted an acting job pretending to be the girlfriend of famous golfer, Eric Vanlare. From their first encounter, she realized he was going to be a handful. He was stunningly handsome and she knew he had amazing hands. She felt out of her depth, inexperienced in love and still a virgin. What seemed like an easy job was going to be more than she had bargained for. Could she concentrate on the job at hand while falling for such a handsome golfer?

CHAPTER ONE
ERIC

Thumping beats pulsed throughout the new club. The intensity of the music created an electrifying motion of energy that could be felt all over. As I looked around, at all the hot bodies, I felt alive. This was certainly the place to be if you wanted to be surrounded by plenty of gorgeous women gyrating all over the floor. I looked over at Matthew, my best friend and winked.

"Pretty cool party, uh?" He yelled over the crowd.

"Yeah, this is awesome," I yelled back.

I was happy to have Matthew by my side that night; he was the guy that could cheer me up , no matter how down I felt. Our friendship went as far back as high school and I could depend on him always, no matter what. He used to be on the golf circuit, but his career took a tumble when he tore his rotator cuff a few years back. We had been playing together all through high school and college. The fact that he couldn't play golf had totally devastated him.. He hadn't let it get him down though; he wasn't the kind of guy that would fall into a depression. He was always laughing, the life of the party and in general, his outlook was always positive.

These days Matthew worked for me. He didn't want to give up on golf. He'd made it his personal mission to make sure that I got to the Masters and he'd succeeded. It was awesome to have a friend like that behind you every step of the way. What more could I ask for? He had agreed to work as my caddie, and having him on the courses with me was beyond what I could ever hope for with regards to a support system. It was certainly more than my father did, though I couldn't discredit the money he'd put into making sure I was a success.

I smiled as a few girls approached our booth and asked if they could come in. We had a private area with bottle service and people had been in and out all night. As the girls started chatting among themselves, Matthew started pouring them some drinks. He looked over at me and I nodded for him to make me another.

"So, your father was harsh with you today?"

"It wasn't him being harsh as much as making it obvious that he didn't want me embarrassing him again on this tour." I said indignantly.

Matthew laughed, "He acts like you do these things on purpose to aggravate him."

"Yeah, I know. Believe me, I want to win more than anything."

"You will buddy, trust me. I have your back and you're going all the way this time. So, what was his whole deal anyways?"

I shook my head, "You wouldn't believe it if I told you."

"Try me."

"He wants me to get a girlfriend. A fake one, and pretend that I'm settling down. He said that I've embarrassed him too much with my 'playboy, party ways,' and that he's cutting me off if I don't do as he says."

"Holy shit man, what are you going to do?"

I frowned, "I'm going to do whatever he wants. I can't get cut off from money man, and it's just until the Masters are over. I just have to put up with him and what he says until then. Apparently, they are bringing in some unknown actress to play my girlfriend."

Matthew laughed, "Are you serious?"

"Yeah, ridiculous, uh."

"Wow, your dad doesn't mess around."

"Nope. So, this is probably going to be my last night as a single guy until the tour is over."

"Well, we better start enjoying ourselves," Matthew said laughing.

As the bottles kept coming, our eyes glazed over from intoxication, and girls came in and out all night long. They were all so beautiful. While on the dance floor I was feeling so free. My feet felt light and the music coursed through my veins. In front of me danced a pretty blonde. She started to unbutton my shirt and I moved my gyrating body closer to her. She was hotter than hell and she had a huge smile on her face.

Miss Blondie and I began sexually tangoing on the dance floor and eventually left the club lip-locked. Several minutes and a taxi ride later, we drunkenly stepped into my apartment. It was a luxury apartment that my father paid for and it was a total chick magnet. Black leather, high tech entertainment, all the amenities of riches with a killer view. She oohed and aahed all over the apartment before I pulled her close to me.

Wrapping my arms around her hot curvy body, I pulled her into me, kissing her aggressively. Our tongues met with fierceness. Her reaction wasn't surprising. She giggled under her breath and I realized she might be thinking we'd be an item after this. They all thought that way. I had a reputation for being a lady's man. She kissed like a freight train though and it made me think of other naughtier things she could do with her mouth. Our tongues were teasing each other and we started ripping clothes off in a heightened fashion. We made a trail of clothing all the way to the bedroom. We started stripping. Her suckle breasts drew me in and I naturally licked using the tip of my tongue invoking a whimpering moan. Her youth showed as she giggled and shivered from anxious energy. She was quite a looker. My body responded instantly. My stylish pants bulging from the throbbing intensity.

I KISSED her again and she eagerly twisted and sucked on my tongue. She was driving me mad and holding back was getting incredibly difficult.

"I want you, Eric," she said with clenched teeth, breathing deeply.

That much was obvious and I was about to give her exactly what she wanted. Her hands caressed my chest, while I took the rest of my clothes off , and then she slid her hands down between my thighs. I looked at her with wanting eyes. She begun to lick my navel. My body trembled and hardened and I led her where I truly wanted her. The edge of her tongue swirling and circling my tip, throwing me into a bodily convulsion. I couldn't help but groan loudly with delight. Even though her seemingly innocent giggles earlier demonstrated her youth; she knew exactly how to massage me into a blissful state. I put my fingers through her silky soft hair and moaned while she satisfied my desire. I wanted to fill her and feel her tighten around me. I gently placed my hands under her chin, moving her upward. This was a surprise to her, but soon she'd feel the surprise of her life.

"Lay back sweetheart," I said breathlessly.

She smiled that beautiful smile and I placed my body on top of her. I could feel the smoothness of her breasts touch my pecs. The throbbing intensified as I slid myself deep inside her. She wrapped her legs around my hips, pulling me closer and the moisture enveloped me. I loved the way she felt. Her warmth was intoxicating. I couldn't get enough of that feeling. Women were incredible beings; they provided so much pleasure. She moaned my name as I thrust smoothly back and forth. With every thrust, I went deeper building up the intensity between us. She moved her legs around my waist as I penetrated her with ferocity.

She was loud and she made it well known how much she was enjoying herself. I smiled down at her, happy that I was bringing her pleasure. There was nothing like looking into a girl's eyes when she was in ecstasy; every thrust brought about more emotions. My body was on the verge, but I was holding back to allow her to climax first. I wanted to explode inside her the moment she was ready. I could tell by her face and her screaming that she had to be close to sharing in our mutual euphoria. I thrust and she cried out. That was it for me. My body jerked with excited release. The buildup was massive and seconds later, I groaned, surrendering my essence into her. I collapsed on her chest and heard that familiar, not so innocent now, giggle again.

CHAPTER TWO

NIKITA

It was Friday night and I was hoping to forget my crushed dreams for the time being. It was just one of those days that I needed to learn to get over and let loose for a little while. I tried making light of the situation, but when it came right down to it, I was devastated that I didn't get the role on the reality show I'd auditioned for. It would have meant everything for my career. For most people, a reality show is nothing special, but for me it would have been a beginning. It was the exposure I needed. What was I thinking quitting school though? The last thing I needed was to prove my parents right. I'd never hear the end of it and that alone was enough to send fear flooding through my veins. I wanted to be a movie star; it was something that I had dreamed of my whole life. I remember at around 5 years old, taking a candlestick, as though it was an Oscar, and standing in front of our little coffee table giving my acceptance speech. My parents knew I wanted to be an actress from that day forward.

I stared at myself in the mirror; noticing the layers of my long brown hair curled around my shoulders. I looked hard into those emerald green hued eyes staring back at me, attempting to change the desperately saddened look into something more positive. People say, 'fake it 'til you make', but wow that was hard to swallow when things weren't going as planned.

"You look great," my sister Mandy said as she peeked her head into the bathroom door.

I smiled at my sister and then looked down at myself. I was wearing a tight red dress that hugged my every curve in all the right ways.

"Thanks, you don't look so bad yourself."

We were planning on going out for dinner and drinks; it was exactly what I needed to get my mind off everything. My sister was always very supportive of my career and I wasn't sure what I would have done without her. Our parents lived in Europe and when I chose to leave, I took Mandy with me. Mandy jumped at the opportunity and considering her job she could work anywhere. Mandy was a freelance writer, which gave her amazing flexibility to work anywhere.

Although we shared the same emerald eyes and brown hair, we didn't look much alike. She took after our father and I more resembled our mother. Her eyes were a bit smaller with shorter lashes, her nose a bit longer, and her lips were a tad thinner. She was still a beauty, but not quite the Hollywood type.

"Let's get going; you're taking forever in there," Mandy said impatiently.

"Well, excuse me, I'm trying not to fall into a depression in here," I said half-joking and half-serious.

"Oh get over yourself, let's get to it."

The great thing about having Mandy as a sister was her straightforward nature. She'd never let me stew in self-pity for very long.

We strolled into the restaurant chatting it up and were

seated rather quickly. As we feasted on an array of appetizers from the local Kelsey's, I started to feel like myself again for the first time all day. I couldn't believe the day I had had, but considering Mandy was with me things were starting to look up.

"Maybe you should start dating someone to get your mind off things."

I laughed, "What are you talking about? That's the last thing I need to do. I don't have the time or the patience. I need to focus on my career, because right now it's falling apart."

"Oh c'mon! It's not that bad. Plus, you'd have probably hated being on reality TV anyways. Just focus on TV and movies for now. Look at Kim Kardashian, do you really want to walk in the footsteps of that train wreck?"

I laughed and then said, "No, that wasn't really my goal, but the thing is, it would have allowed me some exposure and that has certainly launched a few careers," I winked.

"Uh, yeah, who needs it," saying with a fry in hand and a cavalier expression.

She was probably right. As much as I loved the idea of being an actress, reality TV would have completely forced me out of my comfort zone. I guess I just wanted it all too much. Jillian, my trusted agent, was working on new gigs as we spoke and for all I knew I'd be getting a call tomorrow for a new gig, a better gig than the last one.

Just then my phone rang and it showed that it was Jillian. Oh, thank goodness, I hoped she has good news for me.

"Hello," I said with an eager and somewhat chill faking voice.

"Nakita, it's Jillian."

"Oh Jillian, I was just thinking about you, you must have ESP. What's up? Do you have anything good for me?" I had my fingers crossed with anticipation of a possible audition.

"We need to talk. I'd like us to meet for coffee and talk, sooner rather than later?" Her voice sounded rushed and intriguing. I thought this could be promising, but I wasn't quite sure.

I decided to invite her to Kelsey's so we could talk right then. It wasn't long before she arrived at the restaurant and she sat down with a smile on her face.

Jillian adjusted her glasses before saying, "I'm glad this could happen so quickly."

"Yeah, of course. I've been hoping and wanting good news after such a disappointing day."

"Well, I guess that depends on your definition of 'good.'" The quirky smile on her face made me wonder what she was about to offer me.

I laughed, "Great, I can't wait to hear about it."

"Okay, so here it is. I got an interesting call last night and it might be something you would be interested in, but it is unusual. This gig is the first of its kind I've come across."

I nodded, nervously. "Well, let me hear it and we'll go from there."

"Alright." She pulled out her day planner where she had some notes jotted down. After scanning the notes she looked up at me.

"Okay, so here's the deal. There is a pro-golfer in Miami, that is, believe it or not, looking for a fake girlfriend for three months."

"What? That's crazy. What does that even mean? I'm not a hooker for crying out loud, Jillian!" I started feeling anxiety build up. Was this what it was coming down to, I was going to have to take gigs as an escort until I got my big break.

Jillian adjusted her glasses showing her own nervousness, "Hey relax. That's not what I'm talking about here; it's nothing like that. He's not looking for sex. It's an acting job, strictly acting. He basically wants a trophy girlfriend, someone to put on his arm, have pictures taken with, parade around with. It's all a façade, he just needs it to appear as if he has a girlfriend."

I couldn't believe what I was hearing. "Are you sure? You are confident that it has nothing to do with sex, that there are no expectations?" I looked at Mandy and she had a wide grin on her face.

"Absolutely not. I made sure of that when I discussed things with him. He is strictly looking for an actress, someone who can play a role properly, and you can certainly do that."

"Three months in Miami? I guess it could be worse."

"Nope, it's quite hot and mostly sunny days there. You will love it. Not to mention as his girlfriend he will probably wine and dine you quite lavishly."

I nodded, my interest piqued, "How much does it pay?"

She slowly and deliberating said in a higher than usual voice, "Fifty thousand dollars for three months."

My jaw hit the floor. "Holy shit, that's fantastic news." I couldn't believe what I was hearing. "Holy shit."

"I thought you might like that. Money is no object to this guy and I know you can use the money," she said enthusiastically.

"Okay, who is he? I don't know the first thing about golf." My head was whirling with excitement and an overwhelming feeling I couldn't pinpoint.

"Eric Vanlare."

Mandy responded, "Yes, I've definitely heard of him. He's a real player, in more than one sense."

"Yes, well apparently, his father threatened to take his money away if he didn't clean his act up until the Masters were over."

I looked to Mandy, "What should I do?"

"You're obviously going to take it. This could open a lot of doors. You're going to be photographed with someone famous." It was slowly sinking in and I knew this could turn out to be an opportunity of a lifetime.

I turned back to Jillian. "Okay, let's do this."

CHAPTER THREE
NAKITA

It was Saturday and I was flying to Miami on United, first class. I couldn't help but think to myself, you're so crazy, Nakita. A girlfriend to a famous golfer for three months, what in the hell are you getting yourself into. It was all a little insane, but it was also really exciting. When the plane touched down, the butterflies in my stomach went into my throat. I quickly grabbed my carry-on, hurrying off the plane. I couldn't believe how nervous I was.

As I exited the gate I saw a handsome gentleman waiting for me. I knew right away that it wasn't Eric since I had already seen him on video. He was obviously someone important, he carried himself with total confidence and was definitely in charge.

He held out his hand as I walked up to him. I took it and he shook with a firmness that confirmed his character. "Hi, Nakita, I presume? I'm Matthew. I'm Eric's best friend, he asked me to come and pick you up." he said unapologetically.

"Well, it's nice to meet you Matthew. Thanks for picking me up," I said with a nervous giggle. Were all the men in this Sunny State that handsome? First Eric, and now Matthew.

Matthew led her towards a luxurious black Lexus. She could see the all leather interior and it had obviously been washed and waxed recently. He took her bag and opened the front passenger door in a gentlemanly fashion. Sliding into the cushiony soft leather, Nakita felt herself momentarily relaxing.

"We are heading to Eric's home. You will love it there, it's quite beautiful. The estate is well taken care of."

I just nodded, trying to take it all in. I was so nervous to meet Eric and I wasn't sure how it was all going to work.

When we pulled up to the estate, I couldn't believe my eyes. The house, which was more like a mansion was situated overlooking the ocean. The property was vast and lusciously green. The ocean waves could be heard crashing against the shoreline. It was heavenly. Who lived like this? As we rounded the driveway, I noticed the exquisite nature of the front door. Everything was designed perfectly, creating an air of wealth. I tried to shake off the intimidation that I was feeling being in the midst of such affluence and the kind of people I knew I was going to meet.

Matthew came around and opened the door for me in his courteous fashion. I stepped onto the brick layered driveway and followed slowly behind looking all around. As we entered the house, I became overwhelmed seeing the marble floors, lavish furnishings, and incredible artwork hanging from the walls. He brought me into the study where Eric was sitting behind a mahogany desk. He smiled and immediately got up to walk towards me. I was taken aback by the magnitude of his good looks. His body was chiseled, which was well-defined by his fitted grey polo shirt. Photos didn't do him the justice he deserved. His face was distinguished and incredibly handsome. He had big eyes with thick dark eyelashes, a refined nose, and full lips.

"Nakita, it's a pleasure to meet you. I am so happy to have

you come all this way. It must be quite the unusual gig for you," Eric said with a cheerfulness and just a hint of sarcasm.

I grinned and chuckled, "Yes, I have to say I was a little surprised, but also intrigued, as well."

"Good. I just want to say first off I have no interest in having a real girlfriend."

I laughed and then responded sarcastically, "Obviously, that would be why you hired someone to play this part."

Matthew swallowed hard and slightly chuckled, "She got you there, buddy. You're cute Nakita. You will have to keep on your toes with this one."

"Yeah, I guess she told you," Eric started laughing. "I just wanted to make sure things were clear, this is a very unusual situation after all. Even having a fake girlfriend is a whole new experience for me."

"It's no problem. I totally understand."

He smiled and I felt almost faint. It was important to keep my cool though. He had already made things clear, this was to all be an act.

"Let me show you around the property."

"Of course, I'd love to see." I followed him out of the study, walking through a beautifully decorated hallway, and a huge kitchen with an entrance onto the patio. The patio had a large entertainment area with a below ground pool and a sweet gazebo next to it. When you looked outward, the landscaped property went out practically to the ocean front. It was absolutely astonishing. The three of us stopped and sat on the cushioned patio chairs to admire the view. I could definitely get used to this, I thought to myself.

Eric looked over at me and smiled. "So, Nakita you will be living here with me," He asked in a somewhat rhetorical manner.

"Sure, thank you," I said. Of course, I wasn't going to deny an invitation to stay in such a heavenly place.

"We'll put you up in an excellent Airbnb for a few weeks and then we'll set you up here after we officially meet at my favorite club. That will technically be the first time we meet. I will, of course, be behaving myself since that's what I do these days," Eric said jokingly and then laughed.

MATTHEW WAS LOVING every minute of this meeting. It was pretty obvious that Eric and Matthew were close, after all, he was sitting in on a pretty important meeting.

"I will expect you to come on to me Nakita if you think you can handle that." Eric winked at Matthew.

I smiled, "I'm a great actress. Flirting is easy."

"Great."

"So, when is this epic night supposed to be happening?" Matthew interjected.

"Tonight. I would like to get on with things if you know what I mean," Eric said while starting to fidget in his seat getting seemingly restless.

"Okay, I'm in," I said excited by the prospect of standing next to such a hot, rich, and what seemed to be, charming man.

He nodded with a smile. "You won't regret this Nakita. You are going to have the time of your life."

"Well, you might regret this Nakita, but he's not wrong about having the time of your life," Matthew added, with a big grin.

I laughed, "Okay, great."

"You will see a lot of Matthew as well, he is my right-hand man and when I'm working he is my caddy, so we are around each other quite a bit."

"Okay, that's not a problem." Two stunningly gorgeous men by my side, nope, no complaints there I thought to myself.

"Good, he will always be keeping an eye on you, so you don't need to worry about being in a situation that isn't safe for you."

I smiled, "Well, I certainly appreciate that."

"It will be my pleasure Nakita." He winked at me. Oh, I was going to have quite a handful with these two, I could already tell.

"Well, I'm looking forward to working with you guys. It wasn't a job that I expected to ever come up, but it is one that will keep me working until the next gig so I appreciate the chance. I think it's going to be a great opportunity and a lot of fun. I have never been to Miami."

"You will love it here," They both said in unison.

The two guys started making plans while I listened in. My heart was beating a mile a minute, I couldn't believe it was all going down that night. I was cool with it, it was just all happening so fast.

When Eric looked over at me and smiled again, my heart started beating fast again. He was so hot that it was hard to look right at him. It was like looking at the sun. Matthew was going to bring me to an Airbnb that day to get settled in and then I would start to prepare my role for that evening. It had to look authentic and it had to appear as if I was the one hitting on him. He already had a terrible reputation for being a playboy. We all got up to leave and I couldn't wipe the grin off my face even if I'd wanted to.

If you want to continue reading this story, you can get your copy from your favorite vendor by searching for the title:

<u>Love Unexpected</u>

<u>A Fake Relationship Romance</u>

You can also find the e-book version by typing this link in your computer's browser:

https://www.hotandsteamyromance.com/products/love-unexpected-a-fake-relationship-romance

OTHER BOOKS BY THIS AUTHOR

Saving Her Rescuer: A Billionaire & A Virgin Romance

I was just trying to get away from my crazy ex for the weekend when I ended up in a giant pileup on the highway up to Gore Mountain.

https://geni.us/SavingHerRescuer

∿

Sensual Sounds: A Rockstar Ménage

Lust. Lies. Double lives.

The rock and roll industry is full of people who are looking out for themselves and willing to do anything to rise to the top.

https://www.hotandsteamyromance.com/collections/frontpage/products/sensual-sounds-a-rockstar-menage

∿

On the Run: A Secret Baby Romance

Murder. Lies. Fraud. Just another day in the lives of billionaires and women on the run.

https://www.hotandsteamyromance.com/collections/frontpage/products/on-the-run-a-secret-baby-romance

∿

The Dirty Doctor's Touch: A Billionaire Doctor Romance

I am a master. An elitist. I am at the top of my field, and I know what I am doing.

https://www.hotandsteamyromance.com/collections/frontpage/products/the-dirty-doctor-s-touch-a-billionaire-doctor-romance

~

The Hero She Needs: A Single Daddy Next Door Romance

He's the only man I've ever wanted...

https://www.hotandsteamyromance.com/collections/frontpage/products/the-hero-she-needs-a-single-daddy-next-door-romance

~

You can find all of my books here:

Hot and Steamy Romance

https://www.hotandsteamyromance.com

~

Facebook

facebook.com/HotAndSteamyRomance

COPYRIGHT